THE LITTLE DINOSAUR WHO STOMPS IN PUDDLES

Puddles or Lunch?

STORY AND PICTURES BY

ANNA MAKONIN

NUTNAY PRESS

Once, there was a little dinosaur
who loved to stomp in puddles.

She would...
STOMP,
STOMP,
STOMP,
in every puddle.

One day, it rained very hard.
Puddles were everywhere.

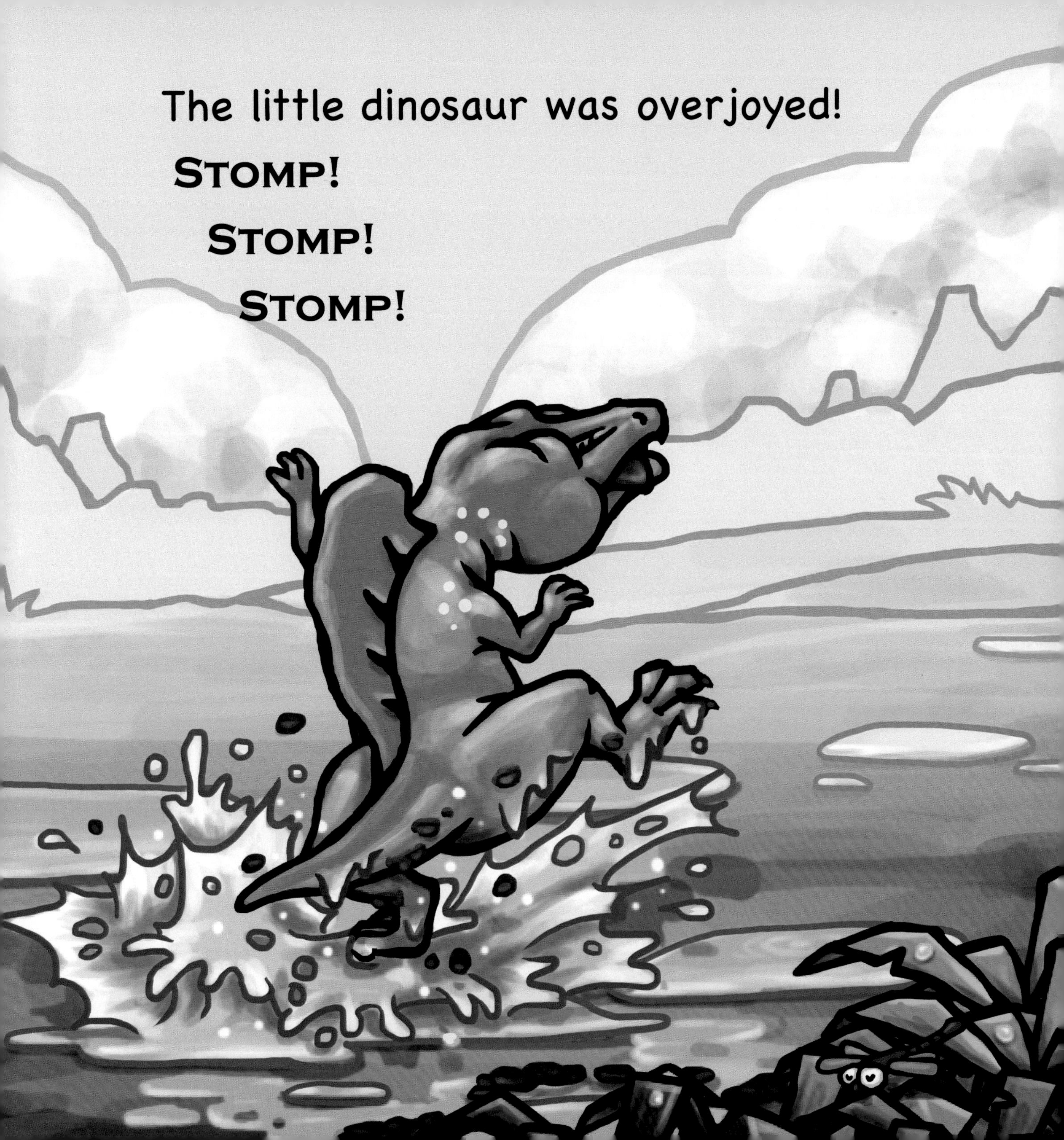
The little dinosaur was overjoyed!
STOMP!
STOMP!
STOMP!

Stomping in all the puddles was hard work.
It made her hungry.

So, she went home for lunch.

Just as she stepped inside the door, Mom said,

"**No!**

No!

No!

Clean your muddy feet first,

then you may come in for lunch!"

The little dinosaur went off to clean her feet.

She came across a pile of rocks.

Would the rocks help clean her feet?

She shrugged and dug her feet into the rocks.

CRUNCH!

CRUNCH!

CRUNCH!

Oh dear, now she had mud and rocks stuck on her feet!

The little dinosaur went on.
She came across a heap of leaves.
Would the leaves help clean her feet?

She shrugged and jumped into the leaves.
RUSTLE!
RUSTLE!
RUSTLE!

Oh dear!
Now she had mud, rocks,
AND leaves stuck on her
feet!

The little dinosaur went on.
She came across some bumps on the ground.
Would the bumps help clean her feet?

She shrugged and rubbed her feet on the bumps.

CRUSH!

CRUSH!

CRUSH!

Oh no! Those bumps were ant hills! Now she had mud, rocks, leaves, AND ants stuck on her feet.

The little dinosaur was getting terribly hungry.

RUMBLE!

RUMBLE!

RUMBLE!

"All I want is to clean my feet so I can have my lunch." She thought.

She tried to claw away the mud, the rocks, the leaves, and the ants from her feet.

SCRATCH!

SCRATCH!

SCRATCH!

Then, she tried to shake away the mud, the rocks, the leaves, and the ants from her feet.

RATTLE!

RATTLE!

RATTLE!

What a disaster!
Now she had mud, rocks, leaves
AND ants all over her body!

Poor little dinosaur.

"I will never clean my feet and will never get my lunch," sobbed the little dinosaur.

BOO HOO HOO!

GURGLE!
GURGLE!
GURGLE!
What was that sound?

She looked for the gurgling sound.
It was a stream of running water!
Would the water help clean her feet?

The water looked cold!
She slowly dipped her foot
into the running stream.

All of a sudden, she slipped and tumbled into the stream!

SPLASH!

SPLASH!

SPLASH!

She quickly got out of the water.
What did she notice?

All the ants were gone!
All the leaves were gone!
All the rocks were gone!
And the mud? All gone!

The little dinosaur was happy
to be clean.
She went home VERY carefully.

Mom gave her a big bowl of fish soup for lunch!
The little dinosaur ate it all up.

SLURP!

SLURP!

SLURP!

After lunch, the little dinosaur went outside to play again.

She came across a big puddle.

Should she stomp in it?

For My Little Dinosaur, Cyan.

-A.M.

For information regarding permission, write to Nutnay Press, info@nutnay.com or PuddlesOrLunch@makonin.com

ISBN: 978-0-9938188-1-3

This book was made possible with the support and contribution by the following wonderful people!

Ah Ma & Ah Ba
Aiden Zachary Mathew - Tyrannosaurus Rex
Alan - Triceratops
Alice Aiden Gawryletz - Pterodactyl
Anders - Pterygotus
Andrea Bellamy - Brachiosaurus
Andrea Chan
Andrus Family - Ankylosaurus, Pteranodon, & T. Rex
Audrey Gawryletz - Therizinosaurus
Austin - Ankylosaurus
Ayomide & Coach - Dino
Bob Gill
Bryan cheng - Tyrannosaurus Rex
Cameron - Tyrannosaurus Rex
Christine Porter Heaney - Hadrosaur
Cole & Olivia - Apatosaurus
Constance - Utahraptor
Cyan Makonin - Therizinosaurus
Daisy and Poppy - Stegosaurus
Darren Schebek - Stegasaurus
David & Christi Zyskowski
Doctor Rainyday - Pterosaur
Dominic Purkiss - Tyrannosaurus Rex
Emily - Stegosaurus
Ethan and Madeleine - Velociraptor
Gabe and Evan - Tyrannosaur
Helen
Emily & Lucas Lin - Purple Dino
J.D. Dresner - Jeholopterus
Judy Lee
Kalvinder Kular
Katy Gerster - Triceratops
Kayla - Pterodactyl
Kayla & Melissa Scott - Velociraptor & Dilophosaurus
Kim Wong
Lisa Yip - Brontosaurus/Apatosaurus
Lowell Orcutt - Triceratops
Lucy Gatiss-Brown - Tyrannosaurus Rex
Luna - Brontosaurus/Apatosaurus
Mabel Chan - Brontosaurus/Apatosaurus
Maia, Sage and Neil - Stegosaurus
Maile Fong - Tyrannosaurus Rex
Mark Slemko - Triceratops
Mary Hoang - Brachiosaurus
Maya Ong
Megan W
Mischa Jovic - Triceratops
Mom & Dad - Velociraptor
Morse Family of Virginia - Tyrannosaurus Rex
OSAAT Entertainment - Tyrannosaurus Rex
Patricia Ho-Asjoe - Brontosaurus/Apatosaurus
Renuka Bhardwaj - Stegasourus
Riha Family - Stegosaurus
Robb N. Johnston
Rod Lowe - Tyrannosaurus Rex
Samantha Skacal
Sarah - Triceratops
Sharon E. Gregson - Baby Ankylosaurus
Stephen Makonin - Epidexipteryx
Suneeta Badhan - Tyrannosaurus Rex
Tabitha "Tabz" Smith - Triceratops
van Ginkel-Fleming family
Wayne khuu - Tyrannosaurus Rex
Wesley Lee - Tyrannosaurus Rex
Westside Montessori Academy, Vancouver - T. Rex
William & George - Therizinosaurus
Winnie Kuan

Special Thanks

Westside Montessori Academy

Ms. C. Williams
Ms. P. Woronko
Ms. B. Stone
Ms. S. Gatiss-Brown

WESTSIDE
MONTESSORI ACADEMY

Mr. K. Kilback

Ms. S. Soares-Almeida

Dr. S. Khan

z
z
z
z